RINGTAIL

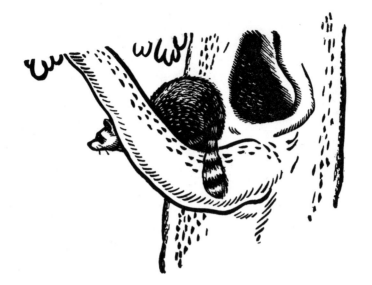

RINGTAIL

by
ALICE CREW GALL
and
FLEMING H. CREW

Illustrated by
JAMES REID

HENRY Z. WALCK, INC.

CONTENTS

THE HOLLOW TREE 11

RINGTAIL MEETS THE SQUIRRELS 17

RINGTAIL LEARNS TO CLIMB 25

THE OUTSIDE WORLD 32

RINGTAIL LEARNS TO FISH 39

THE LITTLE BROWN BAT 46

THE MARSH 54

THE DANGER OF PATHS 63

THE TRAP 71

THE GROUNDHOG'S HOLLOW 80

THE COMING OF THE COLD 90

A CHANGING WORLD 101

BEYOND THE WILLOWS 110

FOR

SALLY AND JOAN

Chapter One

THE HOLLOW TREE

I T WAS an afternoon in early summer, and high
in the hollow of a great old tree Ringtail the little
Raccoon lay curled up on the floor of the family den.

Out in the forest small woods creatures played
about among the trees, or scampered along sunlit
pathways and through the tall, sweet-smelling grass.
Everywhere the birds were singing and the river
sang, too, as it washed gently among the reeds. But
the little Raccoon inside the hollow tree knew
nothing of this busy world around him.

Lying in the darkness of the den, he listened to the
muffled sounds that came to him through the doorway. They were strange, mysterious sounds and they
frightened him a little. He wished his mother would

come and lie beside him and tell him what they meant.

Where was she? he wondered. Always before when he wakened, she had been there lying close to him. But she was not there now.

What if she had climbed down the hollow tree and gone off somewhere? This thought frightened him even more and he called quickly, "Mother! Mother! Where are you?"

The Raccoon mother crossed the den and stood over him, sniffing him anxiously. "Here I am," she said. "What is it, Ringtail?"

"I was afraid you had gone away," he answered, rubbing his nose against her, "but I'm glad you haven't because I want to ask you about the voices."

"What voices? What do you mean, Ringtail?"

"I mean the voices that come in through the doorway," he explained. "Listen, don't you hear them?"

"Yes," she said, "they are the voices of the birds and forest creatures in the Outside World. But do not think about them now, for you must go to sleep again. Look at Little Sister; see how soundly she is sleeping."

Ringtail glanced at his sister, rolled up into a ball of fur beside him, but he was not interested in her just then.

"Tell me more about the birds and forest creatures, won't you, Mother?" he asked.

"Not now," she said gently. "Daytime is the time
to sleep, you know."

"No one else is asleep," Ringtail protested. "The
forest creatures are all awake."

"But they are not Raccoons," his mother told
him. "That is why they are awake; they don't know
any better. Close your eyes, Ringtail."

The little Raccoon closed his eyes obediently, but
he could not sleep. He wanted to hear more about
these creatures who did not know any better than
to stay awake in the daytime. He wanted to ask questions about the forest and the river.

"Mother," he said presently, "I'm tired of staying
in here. Can't we go out and lie on the big branch
for awhile?"

The Raccoon mother looked down at his eager
little black eyes shining through the darkness of the
den. "Yes," she said, "since you are so wide awake
you may as well be out in the sunshine. Come along.
We will go."

Ringtail followed her out onto a great branch of
the hollow tree just below the doorway to the den,
and stood for a moment looking about him.

What an exciting place the Outside World was!

The sunlight danced and sparkled on the river. It touched the leafy roof of the forest and fell in little pools of light upon the ground beneath. And now the voices of the birds and forest creatures sounded cheerful and happy and not at all mysterious, as they had a few moments before.

The little Raccoon settled himself contentedly beside his mother. "Won't you tell me again what I'll do when I am older?" he coaxed. "Begin with me climbing down the hollow tree."

"You will climb down the hollow tree," his mother began, but Ringtail interrupted.

"I'll have to learn how first," he reminded her. "Don't forget to tell about that."

"Yes," she said patiently, "you will have to learn how, for you have never climbed down a tree yet.

But you will go down head first, as all Raccoons do, and when you have reached the ground——"

"I'll go to the river!" Ringtail took up the story eagerly. "And I'll fish for mussels and crayfish and frogs the way you and Father do, won't I?"

"Yes," his mother told him, "you will go down to the river and fish for your supper when you are old enough."

For awhile both of them were silent. The little Raccoon had heard this story many times, but today he liked it better than ever before. Lying there with the warm sun on his back, he thought of the things that he would do when he was ready to go down the hollow tree and off into the Outside World alone.

He would go into the forest yonder and see the strange creatures who lived there. He would go down to the river and fish for his supper; and he would walk through the tall grass on the river bank —the tall grass that waved so gently when the wind blew. All these things he would do when he was older.

Lying quietly beside him, the Raccoon mother looked off across the river to the thicket of low trees and beyond to the far-away hills.

She knew the time was coming soon when Ringtail would no longer be content to stay here on this sunny branch. Young as he was, he was already curious about the world that lay around the hollow tree; and one of these days he would want to go and see it for himself.

There were, she knew, so many things for the little Raccoon to beware of; so many dangers that he did not even dream of! Could she teach him how to guard himself against them? Would he remember not to be too curious about things he did not understand?

The shadows were growing longer now, and the Raccoon mother got to her feet. "I am going back to Little Sister," she said, "but you may stay out here awhile longer if you like."

"By myself?" Ringtail asked eagerly.

"Yes," his mother told him, "you may stay here by yourself if you will be careful."

"I will," Ringtail promised. "I will be very careful." And as his mother reached the doorway of the den he added, "Be sure to tell Little Sister that I am out here all alone. She will be surprised, won't she?"

Chapter Two

RINGTAIL MEETS THE SQUIRRELS

IT WAS the first time that Ringtail had ever been outside the den alone, and he felt very proud as he lay there in the sunshine.

How many things there were to see and wonder about! The clump of willows over there at the bend in the river: what was beyond them? He felt that he could scarcely wait to find out; and he would find out, too, as soon as he was old enough to go down the tree.

He peered cautiously over the big branch. "It is a long way to the ground," he thought, "but I won't mind that when I learn how to climb."

Just then two furry little creatures scampered out of the underbrush and ran straight toward the hollow tree.

Up they came, and out onto the branch where Ringtail lay. But when they saw him they stopped short, their bushy tails arched in the air, and stared at him.

Ringtail had never been so near to any other creature before and he did not know quite what to do. He stared back at them for a moment and then, since they looked like friendly little fellows, he spoke to them.

"Hello," he said.

The two furry creatures did not answer. They only stood there, flicking their tails excitedly, as though ready to scamper back down the tree at a moment's notice.

Presently one of them came a step or two nearer. "Your face is dirty, isn't it?" he said, looking curiously at the little Raccoon.

"No," Ringtail answered in surprise, "my face isn't dirty!"

"Yes, it is," the creature insisted. "It is as black as it can be."

Ringtail was greatly puzzled. Was his face black? he wondered. He must ask his mother about this.

"And I never saw a tail like yours," the creature went on. "It has black rings around it all the way to the very tip. Why is that?"

Ringtail looked at his tail. He had never really noticed it before, but it *did* have black rings around it. Pretty rings they were, too, he thought.

"Well," the creature spoke a little impatiently, "if you don't know why your tail is like that, I don't suppose you know your name either, do you?"

"Of course I do," Ringtail said quickly, glad to be able to answer a question. "My name is Ringtail and I am a Raccoon."

The two little creatures stared at him harder than

ever, but after a moment the first one said, "I know why they call you Ringtail. It's because of your striped tail, isn't it?"

This was a new thought to the little Raccoon and he liked it very much. "Why, of course," he exclaimed, "that must be the reason!"

How many things he was learning today and how fine it was to be talking with someone from the Outside World!

"Where do you live, Ringtail?" the second little creature asked.

"Right here in this tree," he answered. "Do you see that hole there? That's the doorway to our den and I live in there with my mother and my father and my little sister."

"We live in a tree, too," the creature told him. "Our family nest is in the big oak tree in the forest, but we don't stay there much any more. We would rather play around on the ground. Don't you ever play around on the ground, Ringtail?"

"I never have," Ringtail replied. "You see, I'm not big enough yet to climb down the tree."

"Not big enough!" the creature repeated in surprise. "Why you're twice as big as we are! *More* than twice as big!"

For a moment Ringtail could only stare at them,

too confused to make any answer. It was true! He was more than twice as big as they were, and yet they had run up the hollow tree quite easily. He could not understand this at all.

"Well," he said at last, "I am going to learn to climb after awhile. I know that, because my mother told me so. She already lets me stay out here alone," he added proudly.

"I should think she would—a great big thing like you!" said the first creature. "I should think you could go anywhere you wanted to alone. Why don't you?"

"I don't know," the little Raccoon said slowly. "I don't know why I don't."

He wished these two creatures would go away now and leave him alone. He had been glad to see them when they first came, but they had made him uncomfortable and he did not want to talk to them any more until he had asked his mother about the things he did not understand.

Just then, to his great relief, his mother put her head out of the doorway. "Run along home, Gray Squirrels," she said. "The sun is getting low and your mother will be wondering where you are. And you must come in now, Ringtail. Little Sister is awake and it is time for your supper."

The Gray Squirrels scampered off down the tree, chattering as they went, and Ringtail climbed slowly back into the den. But he was no longer proud and happy.

He was bothered about the things the Squirrels had said to him, and not even his supper could make him forget them.

"Mother," he said, when he had had all the milk he could hold, "the Gray Squirrels say I am big enough to climb down the tree. Am I?"

"Not quite yet," she told him. "You must be patient."

"They can climb trees even though they are so small," he said anxiously. "I don't understand about that."

23

"I know," she answered gently. "There are a great many things that are hard to understand. But you will climb when you are ready, Ringtail, so do not think about it now."

"And I'll go to the river and fish, won't I?" he asked drowsily.

"Yes," she said, smoothing his fur softly with her tongue, "you will do that and a great many other things that the Gray Squirrels cannot do."

But the little Raccoon did not hear her, for he was already asleep.

Later that night the Raccoon father and mother slipped quietly away and started toward the river.

"They are growing very fast, aren't they?" the Raccoon father said. "We will soon be taking them along with us when we go to hunt for food."

"Yes," the Raccoon mother answered, "they won't be babies much longer."

The moon was just rising and she stopped for a moment to look back at the hollow tree, standing like a white shadow at the edge of the forest.

Then she turned and went on down to the river to fish for crayfish under the stones.

Chapter Three

RINGTAIL LEARNS TO CLIMB

A ND now each pleasant afternoon Ringtail went out to the great branch below the doorway of the den. Sometimes he went alone, and sometimes his mother came and lay beside him and told him strange things about the forest and the river and the creatures who lived there.

Some of these creatures Ringtail had already learned to know. He knew the Squirrels, and the little brown Chipmunks who darted among the tangled roots of the trees. He knew the old Groundhog who came each day to sit by a great stone in the sun. And he knew the Wren and the Jay and the Woodpecker with its scarlet head.

But there were other creatures, many of them, that

he did not know yet. And as he listened to the things his mother told about them, he felt more and more eager to go into the Outside World and see them for himself.

"Mother," he said one evening when he wakened from a long sleep, "I want to learn to climb down the tree now. May I?"

He had expected that she would tell him he must wait awhile, as she had so often told him before. But to his surprise she said, "Yes, Ringtail, I think the time has come for you to learn."

"Me too!" cried Little Sister. "I want to learn if Ringtail does."

"Very well," their mother said, and going to the doorway she sniffed the air as she always did before going out, "come along then."

The two little Raccoons quickly scrambled out after her.

It was getting on toward dusk and the voices back in the forest were growing quiet, but over by the river the frogs had begun their evening song. They sounded very cheerful, Ringtail thought.

"Now, children," the Raccoon mother said, "I will go down the tree and come up again. Watch me closely and then you may try it for yourselves."

Their little black faces peered eagerly over the

branch as they watched her climb slowly to the ground and back again to where they were standing.

"It doesn't look so very hard," Ringtail said. "I am sure I can do it."

"You go first then," Little Sister told him. "I want to see you do it before I try."

For a moment Ringtail wished he had not spoken so boldly. He was safe up here he knew, but what would happen to him if he should miss his footing on the great trunk of the old hollow tree?

"Come along," his mother urged him. "I will go with you."

The little Raccoon put out a paw and felt the bark

of the tree. Could he do it? Could he trust himself to travel that long distance to the ground?

"Don't forget," his mother reminded him, "you must go down head first and you must dig your claws deep into the bark."

Cautiously Ringtail put out another paw and plunged his little claws as deep into the bark as they would go. Then slowly he started down.

His heart thumped with excitement as he went carefully along. He was doing it! He was climbing down the hollow tree! Soon he would be on the ground where he had wanted to be for so long!

"You did that very well," his mother told him when he had reached the foot of the tree. "And now we will go up again."

"Ho, it's easy!" he said to Little Sister when he was back on the great branch beside her. "You try it now. Mother and I will show you how."

Little Sister was more timid than Ringtail, but at last she ventured down the tree and up again, with her mother and Ringtail close beside her.

"Can't we do it once more?" Ringtail begged.

"No," the Raccoon mother said, "that is enough for today. You will soon do it without any trouble, but you must go back into the den now while I go down to the river and fish."

"I want to fish, too," Ringtail said instantly.

"Not this time," his mother told him. "You must wait awhile for that."

"But I want to taste the juicy mussels that you and Father talk about. I am old enough now to eat mussels."

"So am I," Little Sister urged. "Won't you take us with you, Mother?"

"No," the Raccoon mother said, "I cannot take you to the river tonight. You have only just learned to climb, you know, and you are not ready for the river yet."

The two little Raccoons went reluctantly back into the den and their mother waited in the doorway until she saw them curled up close together in the darkness.

For awhile after she had left them, neither of them spoke.

"It must be fun to fish for your supper," Ringtail said at last. "I wish we could, don't you?"

"Yes," answered Little Sister, "I would like to catch a mussel."

The world around the hollow tree had grown more shadowy and still. The voices in the forest were silent and only the singing of the frogs down by the river broke the evening quiet.

RINGTAIL LEARNS TO CLIMB

Little Sister's eyes were closed now and Ringtail knew by the way her furry sides rose and fell evenly that she was asleep. But he could not sleep.

Getting up very quietly, he went to the doorway of the den and stood sniffing the air as he had seen his parents do. Then, without a moment's hesitation, he stepped outside.

The little Raccoon had had his first taste of adventure and his curiosity was aroused.

He would go and see things for himself!

Chapter Four

THE OUTSIDE WORLD

RINGTAIL'S heart beat fast at the thought of what he was about to do. He was going down the hollow tree *alone* for the first time in his life, and it frightened him a little.

But in a moment he started. Digging his claws into the bark as his mother had taught him, he went slowly along and at last he was safely on the ground.

How different the world looked down here, he thought, gazing about him. Those bushes yonder that had seemed so small when he had looked at them from the great branch overhead were really quite tall. And the river that had seemed so near was a long way off, he found. But these things only added to the excitement of his adventure.

He was here in the Outside World at last. And now he would see the creatures his mother had so often talked to him about.

They were everywhere, she had told him. In the grass and under stones; high in the air and deep in the stream. They were even down in the ground, for there was no nook or cranny too poor to shelter some small life, she had said.

Perhaps some of them were peeping at him right now from the doorways of their tiny homes, and he stood quite still, hoping they would speak to him. But the only sounds he heard were the familiar twilight sounds that he had always known, and so in a moment he started off through the underbrush.

He picked his way carefully, not knowing where he was going and not greatly caring. It was all interesting and wonderful.

Now and then at some sudden sound, the snapping of a twig or the rustle of the wind in the grass, he would stop and listen. But the ripple of water washing gently over stones drew him on, and at last, as he came through a clump of bushes, he found himself close to the river's edge.

What a big river it was! He had never dreamed that it looked like this. And how loud the frogs sounded, now that he was so near to them.

Perhaps he had better run home, he thought, and was about to turn back when a strange voice spoke to him.

"What are you doing here?" it said.

For a moment he was so badly frightened that he could not move. Then the voice came again.

"Here I am," it said, "on the branch right above your head."

Ringtail looked up, and in the gathering darkness he saw an odd-looking creature with a long sharp bill and a tuft of feathers sticking straight up from its head.

The creature must have sensed his fright, for it spoke a third time.

"I am the Kingfisher bird," it said. "You needn't be afraid. I won't harm you."

Ringtail's heart bounded with relief. Of course he was not afraid of birds! They had been all around him since the day he had first gone out onto the great branch, and he was used to them.

"How do you do, Kingfisher bird," he said. "I

didn't answer when you first spoke to me, because I didn't know where you were. I never thought of looking in a tree."

"I see," the Kingfisher said dryly. "Well, now that you know where I am, suppose you answer my question. What are you doing here?"

"I'm just looking around," Ringtail told him.

"Does your mother know where you are?"

"No," Ringtail admitted, "but I don't think she would care."

"Yes, she would," the Kingfisher said. "She would scold you soundly if she knew. You are too young to be out alone. Something unpleasant might happen to you."

"Something—" Ringtail began, but stopped and glanced about him half fearfully.

"Unpleasant!" repeated the Kingfisher.

"What do you mean?" Ringtail asked.

"I mean the Dangers of the river," the Kingfisher

35

said, and the crest on the top of his head rose a little as he spoke. "You should not be out alone unless you know about them."

"Then why don't you tell me about them?" Ringtail asked anxiously.

"I can't," the Kingfisher confessed, "because I do not know what *your* Dangers are. They are so different for each of us. But your mother will know, just as I know my own Dangers, and will tell my children about them when the time comes."

"Oh, have you children?" Ringtail asked eagerly. "How many have you and where are they?"

"I have three," the Kingfisher told him, "and they are safe at home in our burrow."

"Nest you mean, don't you?" Ringtail corrected.

"No," replied the Kingfisher sharply, "I mean exactly what I said. I mean *burrow!*"

Ringtail could not understand this. "But I thought birds built their nests in trees," he said.

The Kingfisher put his head on one side and looked down at him with sharp bright eyes. "Kingfishers don't," he said. "They build their nests in burrows in the river bank. I must be off now," he added, "to find some supper for my children."

So swiftly that Ringtail was startled, the Kingfisher dropped from the branch on which he had

been sitting, and dived with a splash straight down into the river.

He did not go clear out of sight, but rose in the air almost at once. And in his bill he held a small fish!

Ringtail watched him as he flapped slowly away and, for a moment longer, he stood looking off across the river.

The stars were coming out now; the sky was thick with them. But the far-away hills and the thicket were hidden by the night, and suddenly the little Raccoon felt very small and frightened.

The Outside World was not just a friendly place for him to play about in. There were Dangers in it, too! The Kingfisher had said so.

He thought of the warm, safe den high in the hollow tree, with Little Sister sleeping in the darkness. And turning quickly, he ran back through the bushes.

Chapter Five

RINGTAIL LEARNS TO FISH

EVER since the night of his journey to the river, the little Raccoon had felt different.

He was no longer quite contented to lie quietly on the great branch beside his mother. It was no longer enough just to hear about the creatures of the Outside World. He wanted to see them for himself.

He wanted to go into the forest and up to the marsh. He wanted to walk through the tall grass down by the river. And he wanted to fish!

That was really the thing he wanted to do most of all, to fish for his supper, and it seemed to him that he had never wanted anything so much.

He thought of it a great deal and he was thinking of it one afternoon when, from across the den, his father spoke to him.

39

"Ringtail," the Raccoon father said, "would you like to learn to fish tonight?"

"Tonight!" Ringtail got quickly to his feet. "Oh, Father, may I?"

"Yes," his father told him. "You have gone down the tree and off to the river alone. You are old enough now to learn to fish for your supper."

Ringtail could scarcely wait until it was dark. He walked restlessly about the den, now and then looking eagerly out of the doorway. Never, it seemed to him, had the twilight been so long in coming.

But it did come at last, and the Raccoon family set off through the bushes, the Raccoon father and mother walking ahead, with Ringtail and his sister following close behind.

From his perch in a low oak tree, an Owl looked solemnly down at them as they passed along, turning his head slowly to follow them with his great eyes until they were out of sight.

"May I begin to fish right away?" Ringtail asked when at last they stood by the water's edge.

"No," his father said, "you had better watch me first to see how it is done."

The old Raccoon waded out a little way into the stream and began to feel about under the water with

his front paws. Almost at once he returned to the bank holding a fine big clam in his mouth.

"You got one!" Ringtail cried. "You got one, didn't you?"

"I always get one," his father told him quietly. "And now you must watch me closely while I open it. A clam would do you very little good if you did not know how to open its shell and get at the meat inside."

Sitting down on his haunches, the Raccoon father put the clam shell between his teeth and bit the hinge sharply. Then, holding it tightly between his hind paws, he pried it open with his front paws, those paws whose long fingers worked so swiftly and so surely.

"There you are," he said to Little Sister, "there's a fine clam for your supper."

She took it and scooped the meat out with her paw and was just lifting it to her mouth when her mother called sharply, "Wait, don't eat it yet! You must wash it first!"

"Why?" Little Sister looked up in surprise. "Why must I wash it?"

"Because," her mother told her, "that is the right thing to do."

Little Sister eyed the juicy morsel longingly, but

she did as she was told and, taking it to the river, she dabbled it about in the water.

"That is better," her mother said, "and you must remember never to eat your food without first washing it."

"The Squirrels don't wash their food," Little Sister said, swallowing her clam hastily.

"But you are not a Squirrel," her mother reminded her. "You are a Raccoon and must eat as Raccoons do. We always wash our food before we eat it. You must not forget this either, Ringtail," she added.

"I won't forget," Ringtail promised. "And now may I fish?" he asked impatiently.

"Yes," his father said, "you may try it now. But be careful when you feel about in the sand on the bottom of the stream, and do not be in too much of a hurry or——"

"Don't tell me any more," Ringtail interrupted. "I know how."

He waded into the shallow water and began to feel about as he had seen his father do. This was great fun, he thought.

"I've got one!" he cried in a moment. "I've got one!"

But what he had found was only a stone, and he dropped it quickly, hoping no one had seen him.

He looked up to see if Little Sister was watching him, but she was paying no attention to anything except to the food her parents brought her from time to time.

"I'll never get any supper if I don't hurry," Ringtail thought, and forgetting what his father told him about being careful, he began to scrape the bottom of the stream with all his might.

Snap! Something closed over his paw and held it tight.

"Father! Mother! Come quick!" he cried. "Something has hold of my paw!"

He scrambled for the shore as fast as he could, dragging the dreadful thing along with him, while the old Raccoons hurried in from the river and Little Sister jumped down from the pile of driftwood on which she had been sitting.

"It's only a small clam," the Raccoon father said in relief when he saw it. "You got your paw inside its open shell and it snapped shut and caught you.

There!" he said prying open the mussel shell and releasing Ringtail's paw. "It will hurt for awhile, but you will soon be all right again."

"How soon?" Ringtail asked anxiously.

"In a day or so," his father told him. "And the next time you must not be in such a hurry. You had better not try to fish any more tonight," he added. "Just stay here beside Little Sister, and I will bring you your supper."

Ringtail lay down on the sandy beach and licked his throbbing paw, whimpering softly.

Clams, he knew now, were one of the Dangers of the river that the Kingfisher bird had warned him about.

How many more were there? he wondered.

Chapter Six

THE LITTLE BROWN BAT

RINGTAIL'S paw was very sore the next day. It was so sore that when evening came he could not go down to the river with the others to fish.

He limped to the doorway after they had gone, and stood there hoping to see someone he knew. But all the creatures of the woods and stream were either asleep now or busy with their search for food, so after awhile he went back and lay down, feeling very lonely.

"What shall I do?" he thought. "I can't sleep any more because I slept so much today. And there is no one to talk to."

Suddenly he raised his head sharply, for something had fluttered in at the doorway!

He half rose to his feet as he watched it light on

a narrow ledge of wood that jutted out inside the hollow tree, but he lay down again at once. He must not be too hasty this time; it was haste that had got him into trouble with the clam.

So he lay quite still, waiting to see what the little creature would do next.

It did nothing at all, and after awhile Ringtail's curiosity was so great that he got to his feet and limped across the den to get a better view of it.

What a strange little thing it was, he thought, as he walked slowly around and looked up at it.

Its body was covered with fur; and he could see that it had a small mouth with teeth in it and ears that stuck out from its tiny head.

But the strangest thing of all was that it hung from the ledge by its hind legs, its head dangling downward toward the floor!

"Doesn't that hurt?" Ringtail asked.

"Doesn't *what* hurt?" the creature asked in turn, and its voice was so high and thin that he could scarcely hear it.

"Hanging upside down like that," he said. "It doesn't look comfortable."

"It is though," the creature told him.

What should he ask next? There were a great many things he wanted to know.

"You're not a bird, are you?" he inquired.

"Of course not," the creature squeaked. "I'm a little Brown Bat. And now please go away. I want to sleep."

Ringtail did not want to go away. He wanted to stay there and ask questions. He was far less lonely, now that the little Brown Bat had come to keep him company, and he did not intend to let it sleep if he could help it.

"Night isn't the time to sleep," he told it. "I don't sleep at night and neither does my father nor my mother nor my little sister. We sleep in the daytime."

"So do I," answered the little Brown Bat. "I sleep in the daytime and I sleep at night too. I sleep nearly all the time when I am not hunting my food."

"That's queer," Ringtail said.

But the little Brown Bat went on without noticing him: "To tell you the truth," it said, "I have a hard time to get enough sleep. I have a hard time to get enough food, too," it added. "I'm hungry right now."

Ringtail thought about this for a moment. "Then why aren't you out hunting for something to eat?" he asked.

"Because it isn't my time to hunt," the Brown Bat told him. "I have only a little while in which to

catch my food; and when my time is up, I must stop whether I have had enough to eat or not. I often go hungry."

"I'm sorry," Ringtail said, thinking how unpleasant this must be.

"So am I," the little Brown Bat replied, "but you see, I can only catch my food just before dark, and again just before dawn. That's all the time I have."

"Couldn't you find something if you went out now?" Ringtail inquired.

"No," the Brown Bat said, "I couldn't. There aren't many things that I like to eat. Nothing, in fact, but small creatures of the air."

"Birds?" Ringtail asked in surprise.

"No, insects," replied the Bat. "Most of them are so small that probably you have never noticed them; but they have their flying time too. Just now they are all asleep, hidden in the grass; and they won't come out again until just before the dawn. Until then I must go hungry."

"I wouldn't," Ringtail said quickly. "I would go out in the grass and hunt them."

"I can't do that because of my legs," the Bat told him.

"What's the matter with your legs?"

"You ask a great many questions," the little Brown Bat observed, and said no more.

What should he do? Ringtail wondered. If he kept still, the Bat would go to sleep. And if he talked to it, it might fly away and he would never find out about its legs.

He *must* find out about them, he decided. So after a moment he said, "You forgot to tell me what is wrong with your legs, didn't you?"

"Nothing is wrong with them," replied the little Brown Bat. "They are just not made to walk on, that's all. I have a hard time even to creep around on the ground, because my legs are fastened to my wings. And my back legs are bent the wrong way for walking."

Ringtail felt very sorry for the queer little creature who could never walk around on the ground. But in a moment he remembered something.

"You can fly, though," he said comfortingly.

"Yes," said the Bat, "I can fly. Now please be quiet, won't you?"

Ringtail crossed the den and lay down once more. But as he looked at the tiny creature hanging there so still in the darkness, he thought of something else that he wanted to know.

"How long can you hang like that, Brown Bat?" he asked.

The Bat did not answer at once, and Ringtail was afraid it was angry. But after a moment it spoke again.

"Do you know how long winter is?" it asked.

"N-no," Ringtail said doubtfully. "Is it a long time?"

"Yes, it is," said the Bat, "and I hang this way all through the winter. And now you must not bother me any more."

The little Raccoon lay still after this and tried to sleep, but he could not.

The frogs were singing loudly down by the river, and he thought of how much he was missing by not being down there with his parents.

He got up again and went to the doorway and looked out. The willow trees at the bend of the river were silvery white in the moonlight, and he wished more than ever that he knew what was beyond them.

Suddenly, out of the darkness, there came the sound of a voice that he had never heard before—a voice that filled him with terror.

Yap! Yap! Yap! it went, and the fur along Ringtail's back rose stiffly.

He drew his head inside the doorway and waited. The voice was a long way off, for he could hear it only faintly; but he knew, as well as though his mother had told him, that this was another Danger.

And something inside him made him feel that for him it was perhaps the Great Danger!

He stood there trembling and whimpering, straining his ears for the sound of the dreadful voice. But it did not come again.

The night wore on and the Outside World grew hushed and still. And then at last, so softly that he could not be sure he had heard it at all, there came to him the soft note of a waking bird.

The little Brown Bat stirred on its ledge, and quick as a flash it darted out through the doorway and was gone.

Ringtail lay down once more. The night was almost over now and the others would soon be coming back from the river.

Chapter Seven

THE MARSH

FOR a time Ringtail remembered the dreadful baying voice that had frightened him on the night of the little Brown Bat's visit.

He thought of it often at first and always with a prickling feeling along his spine. But after awhile the memory of it faded from his mind and he was once more carefree and happy.

The days were very hot now. Gayly colored butterflies fluttered above the flowering bushes or rode upon the swaying stalk of some tall weed. And yellow bumble-bees droned lazily among the red clover bloom in the meadows.

THE MARSH

This was a wonderful time for the little Raccoon. He went into the Outside World more and more often. Each day that went by, he wandered along new pathways, learning new things.

He knew, almost as well as his father and mother, how to catch crayfish under the stones by the river, and tadpoles and frogs among the water weeds. And he had learned to open the tightly closed shell of a clam and get the juicy morsel of meat inside.

Each night the Raccoon family climbed down the hollow tree and went out to hunt for food; and sometimes they made little journeys along the river bank or back into the forest.

But there were so many things to see and so many places to explore that the nights were much too short for Ringtail, and so, in the late afternoons when the others were still asleep, he would often slip away and wander alone about the river side.

One sultry day when the clouds hung low in the sky, he wakened and went as usual to the doorway and looked out.

A little wind blew through the willows, whitening their leaves, and there was a smell of rain in the air. It was the kind of day he liked best.

As he stood there he could hear the blackbirds chattering up at the marsh. What was the marsh like? he wondered. He had always wanted to go and see it, but there were so many other things to do nearer home that he had never gone.

He would go today, he decided, and climbing down the tree he started off at once, for it was a long way to the marsh and he would have to hurry.

But when he came to the river, the young Musk-rats were splashing about in the water, diving and swimming and having such a good time that he stopped to watch them.

"It must be fun to do that," he said to a little Muskrat who had climbed out on the bank. "You Muskrats are good swimmers, aren't you?"

"We ought to be," the little Muskrat told him, "for we live down yonder in a burrow under the river bank, and we spend most of our time in the water."

"I know," Ringtail said. "I often stop here to watch you. I am on my way to the marsh," he added. "I have never been there yet and I want to find out what is there."

"That's where the old Hermit Muskrat lives," the little Muskrat said.

"Who is he?" Ringtail asked. "I never heard of him."

"You will find out when you get there," the little

Muskrat answered, diving back into the water.

Ringtail started on, more eager now than ever.

Through the orange and yellow jewel weeds he went, through the elder bushes heavy with bloom and through the deep grass, making his way slowly, for there was no longer any path for him to follow.

At last he came to a broad, shallow valley and there, stretching before him, lay the marsh.

The cat-tails and the water weeds grew so thickly all around it that he could only just catch a glimpse of the water. It looked dark and lonely in there, he thought, and he wondered if he could ever find his way out if once he got in.

But he did not stop long to think of this, for as he peered about he saw a path that led across the marsh, and pushing his way through the cat-tail stalks, he started to follow it.

It was a narrow path that wound among the water weeds and rushes. Sometimes Ringtail's feet sank in the soft black mud and sometimes he had to wade through little pools of water. But he kept on, picking his way as carefully as he could.

There must be many creatures living here, he thought, but where were they? Where was the old Hermit Muskrat that the little Muskrat had told him about?

He looked eagerly around him but, except for the blackbirds chattering above his head and an occasional frog who jumped quickly out of his way, he saw no one.

A little farther along the path he came upon a small open place where the cat-tails did not grow so thickly. Here, in the shallow water, a rotting log lay half buried in the bog.

A tiny snake glided quickly into the rushes, but Ringtail paid no attention to it, for on the log he had seen something move!

It looked almost like a stone lying there, but as he looked at it more closely, he saw that it had queer flat little feet and small bright eyes that blinked at him.

"How do you do," he said. "I was just wishing I could see some of the marsh creatures. Would you mind telling me who you are?"

The bright eyes blinked again a time or two before the creature answered.

"I am a Turtle," it said at last.

"I am a young Raccoon," Ringtail told it, "and I have never been in the marsh before. It is a lonely place, isn't it?"

"It is a beautiful place," the Turtle answered. "A very beautiful place."

"But it is lonelier than the river side," Ringtail insisted. "There aren't nearly so many creatures here as there are over there."

The Turtle stretched out its long neck and made an angry hissing sound. "I know the river side," it said. "I was hatched down under the warm sand by the river, and I know it well, but I like the marsh best. There are plenty of creatures here," it added, "if only you know where to look for them. They are everywhere; and down among the water weeds they come and go and are never still!"

"I don't see them," Ringtail said, looking down at the water. "Why don't they——"

He stopped short, staring in amazement. The Turtle was still lying on the log just as it had been, but its head and feet had disappeared from view. It was now only a round flat object that looked more than ever like a stone.

"Oh, Turtle," Ringtail cried, "your head and feet are gone! Where are they?"

"They are in my shell, of course," the Turtle answered.

"In your shell!" Ringtail was so astonished that he could scarcely speak.

The Turtle poked its head out, pleased that it had startled the young Raccoon. "Yes," it said, "I can draw them into my shell whenever I like. I always do it when I am in danger, or when I do not want to be annoyed," it added, looking at him sharply.

Ringtail was a little embarrassed by this. "Do you mean that I have annoyed you, Turtle?" he asked.

"Well, I don't like to hear you say the marsh is lonely," the Turtle told him.

"Oh, I'm sorry!" Ringtail said. "I only meant that it seemed lonely here until I met you. There's someone else that I want to meet, too," he went on, "the old Hermit Muskrat. Do you know him?"

"Of course I know him," answered the Turtle. "He loves the marsh as well as I do and he will never leave it."

As he finished speaking he began to creep slowly and awkwardly down along the log.

"Wait!" Ringtail cried. "Please don't go away, Turtle! Won't you tell me where I can find the Hermit Muskrat?"

But the Turtle went on as though he had not heard, and then silently he slid from the log into the water and was gone.

Chapter Eight

THE DANGER OF PATHS

A FEELING of loneliness came over the little Raccoon as he stood looking at the empty log. Far off down the river he could hear the cry of the Kingfisher, and for a moment he wished he were back in the hollow tree with his father and mother and little sister.

But his encounter with the Turtle had given him fresh interest in the marsh. "I won't go back just yet," he thought, and started on.

He had gone but a little way farther when something in the path just ahead caught his eye.

It lay half hidden by the tangled roots of the water

weeds, so that Ringtail could not see it clearly. He
went quickly forward, hoping it might be another
marsh creature, and it was not until he got quite
close to it that he saw its two wide-open jaws, each
with a row of sharply pointed teeth!

For a moment he was badly frightened, but the
thing lay there so quietly that he grew a little curious
about it. It could not be unfriendly, he thought,
since it did not stir at his approach, and going a step
or two nearer, he put out a paw to touch it.

But just in time he remembered that his mother
had often warned him not to be too curious about
the things he did not understand, and he drew back
quickly.

"No," he said, "I had better not touch it." And
stepping very carefully he crept past it and went on,
not knowing that this quiet thing at the edge of the
path was one of his greatest Dangers!

Soon he forgot it altogether, for now the sun
shone through a rift in the clouds and he caught the
glint of blue water through the cat-tail stalks.

Pushing his way through the reeds, he saw before
him an open bay. Close to the edge of it rose a little
island of dry ground, and on this island sat an old
Muskrat, chewing the ends of a water plant.

"It's the Hermit Muskrat!" Ringtail thought, his

heart beating fast with excitement. "What a big old fellow he is! He doesn't see me; he doesn't know there is anyone near him. I will hide here in the rushes for awhile and see what he does."

But the old Muskrat only kept on chewing the water plants.

For a long time he did this until he had eaten his fill. Then, turning himself about so that he faced the clump of rushes in which Ringtail was hiding, he said quietly:

"I see you in there, young Raccoon. I knew you were there as soon as you came. What do you want?"

"I don't want anything," answered Ringtail, coming out of the rushes at once. "I'm just walking about to see what I can see. But how do you know who I am?" he asked curiously.

"By your black face and your striped tail, of course," the old Muskrat answered. "You are a long way from home, aren't you?"

"Yes," Ringtail said, "I live in the hollow tree by the river."

"I know that tree," the old Muskrat told him. "I have seen it many times."

"It's nice over there, isn't it, Muskrat?"

"Yes," answered the Muskrat, "but I like the marsh best. If you will turn your head a little, you will see my house yonder at the edge of the bay."

Ringtail looked, but all he could see was a mound of cat-tail stalks and twisted reeds rising above the water.

"Is that your house?" he asked in surprise.

"Yes, it is really my winter home," explained the old Muskrat, "and you can only see the top of it. The rest is under water."

"But don't you live in a burrow?" Ringtail asked. "The young Muskrats at the river do."

"I used to live in a burrow," the old Muskrat replied, "and I still have one over at the river; but I don't stay in it much any more."

Ringtail looked again at the Hermit Muskrat's house. There was something wrong with it, but he couldn't think what it was.

"Oh, I know!" he said after a moment. "It hasn't any door."

"Of course it has a door," the Muskrat answered, "but the door is under water, and you can't get in unless you are a good diver! The part of my house that you see is my upper room, and it is as snug and dry as your den in the hollow tree. Tell me," he went on, "how did you get here, young Raccoon?"

"Through the cat-tail stalks," Ringtail told him. "I came along a path that I found."

"That's my path," the old Muskrat said. "I made it."

"Did you?" Ringtail looked at him in admiration. "Well, it's a fine path. I couldn't have got here without it."

"No," the old Muskrat said gravely, "you couldn't." And then for a moment he was silent, nibbling thoughtfully at the end of a water plant.

"Do you often wander about the marsh alone?" he asked presently.

"No," Ringtail told him, "this is the first time I have ever been here. But I will come often now that I have found the way."

"If I were you," the old Muskrat lowered his voice and glanced about him, "if I were you, I would be very careful about following paths."

"Why?" Ringtail lowered his own voice, for the Muskrat's words frightened him a little.

"Because they are dangerous," the Muskrat said. "They are *very* dangerous. I know!"

Another Danger! Ringtail felt the prickle along his spine, but in a moment he asked, "What could a path do to me, Muskrat? I don't see how it could hurt me."

The old Muskrat seemed about to speak, but instead he rose to his feet and took a few halting steps. And Ringtail saw that he was lame!

"I have lost a foot," he said simply.

The little Raccoon stared at him in terror. "Did it hurt much, Muskrat?" he asked at last.

"At first it did," the Muskrat told him, "but not now."

"How did it happen?" Ringtail asked.

The old Muskrat came a step or two nearer. "It happened," he said slowly, "on a path!"

For an instant Ringtail remembered the strange object he had seen lying in the path a few moments before. But he was too much interested in the old Muskrat to think of it any more just then.

"I don't often speak of it," the old Muskrat was saying, "but I think I will tell you about the day I lost my foot. You are young and it will be well for you to know about the Dangers of paths."

He lay down on the ground and folded his hurt leg under him as though to hide it from sight.

"Lie down, young Raccoon," he said. "It is a long story."

Chapter Nine

THE TRAP

"A LONG time ago," the old Muskrat began, "when I was young like you, I lived with my family in a burrow in the river bank, not far from your hollow tree.

"I had many brothers and sisters; so many, in fact, that our mother did not even try to keep an eye on us, and we did much as we pleased.

"I used to wander alone in search of food, and my favorite spot was the marsh—this very marsh. I liked it then as I do now because it is here that the lily roots and water weeds grow thickest.

"One summer morning I set off alone as usual,

intending to come up here and have a fine meal. But the air was so warm and inviting that I decided to go first to the forest and see what I could see.

"I knew many of the forest creatures and liked to talk with them. But on this particular morning, although I walked on and on, I saw no one. The forest seemed to be deserted.

"I was wondering about this when a Jay screamed at me from a branch overhead. 'You had better go back to the river as fast as you can, Muskrat,' he called loudly. 'You are not safe here.'

"Before I could ask him why, he flew away, and as I stood there I could hear his warning cry far in the distance.

"Should I go home, I wondered, or was the Jay only trying to frighten me?

"The stillness decided me. I would go home.

"I started back along the path, but I had not gone far when I heard a voice echoing through the forest. Yap! Yap! Yap! it went, and my heart stood still with fright."

Ringtail's heart stood still, too, as he remembered the voice he had heard on the night of the Brown Bat's visit, and he half rose to his feet. But the old Muskrat went on speaking as though he had not noticed.

"The voice was new to me," he said, "and I feared it. So as quickly as I could, I hid myself in a clump of bushes.

73

"In a moment it came again, this time nearer than before, and I caught a glimpse of a shaggy creature, its nose close to the ground, running through the bushes. But it disappeared quickly, and I saw that it was not hunting me but some forest creature."

"Then did you run home?" Ringtail asked.

"No," the Muskrat told him, "for as I hid there in the bushes I heard *another* voice."

"Who was it?" Ringtail moved a little closer to the old Muskrat. "Who was it you heard?"

The Muskrat paused a moment before replying. "It was the Mighty One," he said.

"The Mighty One!" Ringtail exclaimed. "I have never heard of him. Who is he?"

"I cannot tell you that," the Muskrat answered, "for I do not know myself. He is not a creature like you and me, but is tall and straight and walks on two legs."

"Is he a Danger?" Ringtail asked quickly.

Again the old Muskrat hesitated. "Yes," he said at last, "I think he is. I do not like to talk of him because he is too mysterious, but I know that sometimes he walks in the forest and the shaggy creature is always with him. It belongs to him and obeys him."

"How do you know, Muskrat?"

"I know," the Muskrat replied, "because on this day when I was hiding in the bushes, I heard him call to the shaggy creature, and it came running back to him. Though it was far off in the forest, it came back to him at once. That is why I call him the Mighty One, because the shaggy creature belongs to him and obeys him."

"What did they do when the shaggy creature came running back?" Ringtail asked.

"They went away," the Muskrat answered. "I heard them going through the underbrush. For a while I did not dare to stir, and then at last I heard the forest creatures begin to move about again, and I felt less terrified. They too had been hiding; that is why the forest had seemed deserted. But since they were coming out again I felt that it would be safe for me to leave my hiding place.

"By this time I was very hungry and thought of the lily roots up at the marsh. I would go there now, I decided, and eat my fill of them. And I started cautiously off along the path.

"All at once I smelled food and I ran quickly forward to find it. The weeds were trampled where the Mighty One had walked, but the food was there. I could smell it plainly.

"I put out a paw to push aside the tall grass, and

as I did so, something sprang up and caught my foot!

"At first I thought it was some creature who had seized me. But as I fought to free myself I could feel that it was hard, as hard as stone. There was no creature who felt like this, I knew."

A little whimper rose in Ringtail's throat. "What *was* it, Muskrat?" he asked. "What had caught you?"

"I believe," the Muskrat's voice sank almost to a whisper, "I believe it was something that the Mighty One had hidden there to catch me or some other hungry creature who would be drawn to the spot by the good smell of food."

"Oh, no!" Ringtail cried out. "Surely he would not do that!"

"I think so," the old Muskrat said slowly. "I think so. The hard jaws bit into my leg deeply," he went on after a moment, "and I was almost wild with pain. I was so frightened that I scarcely knew what I was doing, but I kept on biting and gnawing as hard as I could, for I knew that I was fighting for my life.

"I even called to my mother to come and help me, but she was in our burrow at the river and could not hear me.

"Squirming, twisting, and biting, I made one last effort. And suddenly I found that I was free!

"How I got back to the river I do not know to this day, but I did. And diving in, I swam straight for home.

"It was hard for me to swim, though I did not understand why then, and it was not until I had dragged myself into our burrow that I knew my foot was gone.

"I had left it in the hard thing hidden in the path, the thing with the cruel sharp teeth. But I had escaped with my life, and I was thankful."

"Poor Muskrat," Ringtail said softly. "It must have hurt."

"At first it did," the Muskrat repeated, "but not now. My mother cared for me until my leg was well, and though I could never again run as easily as before, I learned to get about, as you see."

He rose to his feet and stretched himself. "It is almost evening," he said, "and you must be getting home."

"Yes," Ringtail answered, "I must go. Thank you for telling me your story, Muskrat. I won't forget it."

"All right, see that you don't," the old Muskrat said, and limped off down toward the water.

THE TRAP

As he reached the edge of the bay he turned and looked back at Ringtail. "And if I were you, young Raccoon," he said again, "I would be very careful about following paths."

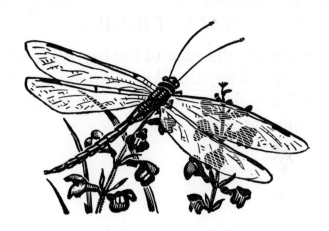

Chapter Ten

THE GROUNDHOG'S HOLLOW

ON A hot, still summer morning, the Kingfisher sat on the dead branch of a tree close by the river and looked down at the water.

He had finished his breakfast and now he was watching a blue Dragon Fly as it darted about. For a time it interested him, but presently it came to rest on the tip of a water weed, and the Kingfisher, feeling drowsy, was about to close his eyes when suddenly he cocked his head on one side and listened intently.

From off beyond the far-away hills came the low rumble of distant thunder. A little puff of wind stirred the willow trees, and then all was still again. The Kingfisher hopped farther out along the branch. "There is something in the feel of things this morning that I don't like," he said. And as a nearer rumble of thunder broke the stillness, he dropped swiftly from the tree and flew away.

A flash of lightning zigzagged across the sky. The trees of the forest swayed in the rising wind. Great drops of rain began to fall and the thunder echoed along the valley.

High in the hollow tree, Ringtail lay and listened to the storm. He was too excited to sleep and now and then he would go to the doorway and look out at the sheet of driving rain, falling so heavily that it hid the forest world from his sight.

The long day dragged by and still the rain beat down, and the wind tore at the hollow tree until it shook and trembled. But when evening came, the storm quieted and at last the Raccoon family started out to look for food.

"We cannot go down to the river," the Raccoon father said when they reached the foot of the tree, "for the river is swift and angry. We must find our food in the forest tonight."

"But what *can* we find to eat in the forest?" Ringtail asked anxiously.

"There will be grubs," his father told him, "that we shall dig from under the roots of old trees, and there will be insects. There will be berries, too, and these things must be our food until we can go to the river again. Come along. There is no time to lose."

Keeping close together, they made their way silently through the darkness.

It was a fine adventure, Ringtail thought, to be in the forest on a night like this. Great branches, broken from the trees, lay strewn about upon the ground; and many river creatures, driven from their homes by the storm, scurried along the byways or hid themselves in trees and bushes, bewildered by their strange surroundings.

The night passed all too quickly for the little Raccoon. And when the next day, and the next, and for many days after that, the river was too muddy and swollen for them to fish in, he went eagerly back to the forest to walk among the trees, or peep out from the tall grass and weeds at the strange things going on around him.

His mother had warned him against wandering off alone, but there were so many things for him to see that he soon forgot her words. And each day found him going deeper and deeper into the forest.

One afternoon when the sun was low in the sky, he set off along a path that he had long wanted to follow. It was a dark path that wound among tall weeds and bushes, and Ringtail did not know where it led.

But he had not gone far before he came upon a little hollow whose steep sides were covered thickly with underbrush. Great stones lay tumbled in confusion all around; and beneath a shelf of rock were shadowy caverns and curious holes, dark and mysterious, that ran deep into the ground.

"What a queer place," he thought. "Who lives here, I wonder?"

As if in answer to his question, a voice spoke to him from somewhere in the darkness.

"Do you see them, young Raccoon?" it asked almost in a whisper.

Ringtail was startled, but in a moment a furry head looked out from a hole under a rock, and he saw that it was the old Groundhog who came each day to sun himself near the hollow tree.

"Oh, it's you, Groundhog," he said. "What are you doing here?"

"I live here," the Groundhog told him, coming a little farther out of his hole and looking anxiously around. "This is my home."

"What's the matter?" Ringtail asked. "Has something frightened you?"

"Yes," the Groundhog said, "there is a Danger in the forest."

"A Danger!" Ringtail exclaimed. "How do you know?"

"I saw it," replied the Groundhog, "back among the trees."

"I saw it, too," a Chipmunk said, coming out from behind a stone, "a great shaggy creature running swiftly with its nose to the ground. I saw it, and so I darted in here——"

"There are two Dangers!" another voice said, so close to him that Ringtail jumped a little. It was the Rabbit and its great eyes were filled with alarm. "There are two Dangers, I tell you! The shaggy creature and another who is tall and straight and walks on two legs!"

"That must be the Mighty One," Ringtail said, drawing back into the shadow of the rocky shelf, "and you are right, he is a great Danger."

"It is the shaggy creature that I fear most," the Chipmunk said. "The shaggy creature who runs on four legs and looks so fierce."

"He is surely not so fierce as the Great Owl!" a tiny Fieldmouse cried, peeping timidly out from under a fallen tree. "The Great Owl is the one *I* fear."

"The Great Owl is asleep now," the Chipmunk said impatiently, "but these two are walking in the forest. I saw them."

"Why do you call him the Mighty One, young Raccoon?" the Groundhog asked. "Is it because he is tall and straight and walks on two legs?"

"The old Muskrat of the marsh calls him that because he is mysterious," Ringtail explained, "and because the shaggy creature belongs to him and obeys him."

"And loves him, too!" the Rabbit added, hopping a little nearer to the old Groundhog's hole. "I have seen them together and the shaggy creature *loves* the Mighty One—as you call him—and obeys him whenever he speaks."

"The shaggy creature is the one who hunts us out," the Chipmunk insisted. 'He runs through the forest with his nose to the ground and tracks us to our holes. He is the worst!"

"No," said the Rabbit, "the one who walks on two legs is the worst, because he carries the strange shining stick."

"The Great Owl with the long sharp claws is the worst of all!" said the tiny Fieldmouse. "Why should you fear a shining stick?"

"I will tell you why I fear it," answered the Rabbit. "It is because this stick can kill from a long way off!"

At these words the Fieldmouse scampered quickly back into the darkness.

"Are you *sure*, Rabbit?" Ringtail asked, almost in a whisper. "How can it do that?"

"I am sure," the Rabbit told him, its great eyes more frightened than ever, "because I have seen it.

Once in the forest when I was hidden in the weeds, I saw the Mighty One raise the shining stick in his two paws. There was a loud noise, and then from a tree a little Gray Squirrel fell down to the ground. The shining stick had killed it from a long way off."

None of the creatures spoke for a moment after this, and Ringtail, looking out from the shadow of the rock, thought of the hollow tree and wondered if he would ever get back to it again.

"Listen!" the Groundhog said, and as he spoke they heard the baying voice of the shaggy creature far in the distance.

Quick as a flash the other creatures hid themselves away, and Ringtail, waiting only a second, ran to the hemlock tree at the edge of the hollow and did not pause until he was high among its branches.

For a long time he lay there, not daring to move, his bright black eyes darting this way and that, his ears strained for any sound.

And then, just as the last rays of the setting sun faded from the sky, he saw them!

The Mighty One, tall and straight, came out of the forest with the shaggy creature trotting by his side.

The little Raccoon crouched low behind his screen of leaves and watched them as they went along the river path and disappeared around the clump of willows. Then he got slowly to his feet.

He could go back home now, back to the hollow tree. He had seen the Mighty One, and the shaggy creature whose voice had frightened him in the night so long ago. But they had not seen him!

He had come safely through another day.

Chapter Eleven

THE COMING OF THE COLD

THE sky was beginning to turn gray with the first pale light of morning when the Raccoon family returned to their den after another night spent in the forest.

The Raccoon father did not lie down at once as he usually did but stood for awhile, looking out at the doorway, and presently Ringtail came and stood beside him

"What are you looking at, Father?" he asked curiously.

"I am looking at the river," the old Raccoon told him, "and I think that tonight we can go down and fish for our supper. We will spend no more nights in the forest; the river is ready for us now. It is no longer swift and angry."

"Oh, I am glad!" exclaimed Ringtail. "We have been away from it a long time, haven't we?"

"It has seemed long," the Raccoon father answered, "and it will be good to get back to it again."

"I like the forest," Ringtail said thoughtfully. "I like to walk about among the trees and watch the forest creatures in their homes. But I like the river best."

"We all do, we Raccoons," replied his father, "for the river is more friendly to us than the forest."

"It is, isn't it?" Ringtail said. "And I like to live close to it, here in the hollow tree."

"You will always live close to the river, Ringtail," his father told him. "Even when you are older you will never go far away from it."

"Won't I always live in this hollow tree?" Ringtail asked.

The Raccoon father looked down at the little fellow standing beside him. "We will not talk about that now," he said gently, "for we must sleep. The daylight is already here."

Ringtail lay down and closed his eyes. Of course he would always live here in the hollow tree, he told

himself. He would never want to live anywhere else. And how glad he was that he could go down to the river tonight and fish for mussels! He would wade out into the shallow water, he thought sleepily, and feel about on the bottom of the stream——

He wakened with a start. His father and mother were already stirring and Little Sister was whimpering softly at being roused.

"Come, Ringtail," said his mother, "it is growing dark. You have had a long sleep, and it is time now to go out and hunt for food."

The little Raccoon felt a thrill of excitement at the thought of going back to the river; and as he trotted along behind his parents with Little Sister at his side, he looked eagerly around at the familiar landmarks he had so often passed.

They were all here: the low oak tree where the Great Owl lived, the bushes, the underbrush, and the tall grass in the open place by the river. The storm had not hurt them at all.

They would always be here, he thought, just like this!

The rising moon made a shining yellow path across the water as they came to the river bank, and Ringtail, wandering a little way from the others, stood very still and looked about him.

The river again flowed peacefully along as it had on that first night when he had come down to it to fish. Everything was the same.

But no, not quite the same either. For there was a new sound in the air tonight, the small shrill sound of tiny creatures who sang and sang and never stopped.

Who were they? he wondered. And why did they make him feel suddenly a little lonely?

"Ringtail!" It was his mother's voice that called him.

"Here I am," he answered, walking up the bank to meet her.

"What are you doing?" she asked. "You should be fishing for your supper."

"I am listening to the new voices in the grass and trees," he told her, "and wondering what they are."

"They are the voices of little creatures who come for awhile each year," his mother answered, "and sing the whole night through until——"

"Until what, Mother?"

"Until something happens to make them stop their singing," she finished.

Ringtail looked at her questioningly. "What is it that happens?" he asked.

"It is the Coming of the Cold," she told him.

"There is not much singing time left to them now, for the summer is nearly done."

"And then what will happen?"

The Raccoon mother did not reply at once. "Have you seen the Tulip Tree of late, Ringtail?" she asked presently.

"The Tulip Tree!" he said in surprise. "Yes, I have seen it. Its leaves have changed their color, haven't they?"

"And soon they will drop to the ground," his

mother told him. "Then the little creatures in the grass will stop their singing and the snow will come and cover the bare branches of the trees. And winter will be here."

"Tell me about winter, Mother," Ringtail said. "Will I like it?"

"You will be asleep and will not know about it, Ringtail," she said. "We will all be asleep, close together in our den. And we will not mind it when the wind blows down from the hills and whistles through the trees. We will not mind it even when the river is cold and still and we cannot fish for mussels any more."

"The river!" Ringtail said sharply. "Will something happen to the river, when winter comes?"

"Yes," said his mother, "the river and the marsh will be covered with a hard cold roof that you can walk on, as you walk on the ground. And you can look down through this roof and see the water below!"

"But I won't see it or walk on it, for I'll be asleep," Ringtail said in disappointment.

"It may be that the roof will still be there when you wake up," his mother told him. "I myself have seen it after the long sleep. But it soon goes away when the warm sun shines on it."

Ringtail thought about this for a moment. "Will the old Muskrat of the marsh be asleep, too?" he asked.

"No, the old Muskrat will not sleep," his mother said.

"But if there is a hard cold roof over the river and the marsh, how can he find his lily roots and water weeds?"

"I will tell you something very curious, Ringtail," his mother answered. "The Muskrats can swim about *under the hard cold roof of the river!* I know this is true, for I have seen them do it."

"That is strange," Ringtail said wonderingly. "And will the old Muskrat of the marsh find his lily

roots and water weeds just the same down under the hard cold roof?"

"He will find them," she said. "The old Muskrat will not go hungry."

The little Raccoon looked out across the river at the yellow path of light. "When winter comes," he said slowly, "the Muskrats will swim about under the hard cold roof of the river. The little Brown Bat will hang with its head down all winter long. And I'll be asleep in the old hollow tree."

"Yes," answered his mother, "that is what will happen, Ringtail."

"I wish I did not have to sleep," he said wistfully. "Why do I?"

"It is the way of Raccoons," his mother said. "I cannot tell you *why* we do it. I only know that we do."

"But I want to see the winter," he told her. "I want to see all of it!"

"You will not want to when the time comes," she comforted him. "You will be glad enough to sleep."

"Are you sure?"

"I am sure, Ringtail."

For awhile neither of them spoke again. A little wisp of cloud floated across the face of the moon and back in the forest they heard the Great Owl's lonely cry. But the tiny creatures in the grass and bushes sang bravely on.

"Mother," the little Raccoon said suddenly, "I want to fish now. I want to fish in the river for my supper while I can!"

Chapter Twelve

A CHANGING WORLD

THE early mornings were now crisp and cool. At times, a white frost touched the grass and the bushes and there was a keener edge to the wind that came down from the hills.

But the afternoons were still warm and pleasant, and Ringtail spent long hours stretched out upon the great branch of the hollow tree in the sunshine.

Today, as he lay there, he saw a world that was changing—changing so slowly that it could scarcely be noticed from day to day, but changing surely, just as his mother had told him it would.

The trees were now all gold and scarlet, and little showers of leaves fell to the ground each time the wind stirred among them. A thin blue mist hung in the air and the hillsides and meadows were yellow with goldenrod.

How soon would winter come? he wondered. And what would it be like when it got here?

Neither his father nor his mother could tell him much about this. The old Groundhog could not tell him either; nor the Chipmunks. He had asked them all but they only said that winter was a cold and dreary time, a time to lie asleep in a snug den or burrow.

There was so much he wanted to know. What had become of the birds—the robins, the catbirds, the finches and the orioles? A few of them still lingered here to feed on the red seeds of the sumac tops and the thorn apples that grew at the edge of the thicket. But where were the others?

It was very still without them, and without the little creatures who had sung in the grass the whole night through. He wished he might hear these little creatures once again, and raising his head he listened intently. But the deep "chur-ump" of a bullfrog down in the rushes was the only sound he heard.

Suddenly a thought came to him. The old Hermit Muskrat could tell him about the winter. Of course he could! Why hadn't he thought of him before?

Getting to his feet, he climbed down the hollow tree and started off to the marsh.

The old Muskrat was busy fastening some rushes in the roof of his queer house in the bay. "Good day, young Raccoon," he called when he saw Ringtail. "I am getting everything snug and tight for winter."

"Winter!" Ringtail said. "That is what I have come to talk to you about. Won't you please tell me what winter is like, Muskrat?"

The Muskrat stopped his work for a moment. "It is a cold and dreary time," he said briefly.

"I know that already," Ringtail told him, "but there are a great many other things that I want to know about it."

The old Muskrat slipped into the water and swam across to where Ringtail was standing on the little island of dry ground. "What is it you want to know?" he asked, lying down and folding his hurt leg under him. "I will tell you anything I can."

"Well," began Ringtail, "I want to know first about the Kingfisher bird. He does not come any more to sit on his dead branch by the river, and I wonder why."

"He has gone away," the Muskrat replied, "and all through the winter he will not come again to the tree by the river."

"Is he in his snug burrow in the river bank?" Ringtail asked.

"No," said the Muskrat, "he is not there. He has gone with the others and they will travel far. They have been going for many days—all the birds—and now even the blackbirds no longer chatter here in the marsh. Soon the forest creatures will go to sleep, and then——"

"You will not sleep, will you, Muskrat?" Ringtail interrupted.

"No," the Muskrat said, "I will be awake all winter long."

"Will you like that?"

"I won't mind," the old Muskrat replied. "It will be cold and lonely, and food will be very hard to get. Only down under the roof of the river shall I find my lily roots and water weeds. But I will not mind, for I am used to it."

"If winter is such a cold dreary time," Ringtail said, "I should think you would rather sleep until it is over."

"Who would look after my marsh, if I were asleep?" the old Muskrat asked. "Or my house? Or my path?"

"That's so!" exclaimed Ringtail. "I hadn't thought of that. If you are awake you can watch them all winter and see that nothing happens to them!"

"Yes," the Muskrat said, "I can watch them."

"I hate to think of you being lonely," Ringtail said after a moment.

"You must not think of that," the old Muskrat told him kindly, "for the winter will pass. And when it does, they will all come back; the birds and forest creatures. The blackbirds will chatter again in the marsh and the frogs will sing along the river bank. There will be greening rushes then, and I will be the first to see them!"

There was a note of gladness in the old Muskrat's voice as he said this, and Ringtail, catching something of his excitement, said quickly:

"And I'll go to the river again and fish for mussels! I'll come up here to see you, too. And you will be here on your little island waiting for me, won't you?"

"I will be here," the Muskrat said, "but there will be much for you to do when you waken, and many things for you to think about besides visiting with an old Muskrat. It will be a busy time along the river, with nests to be built and burrows to be dug in

the river bank. Those who live in dens will be scurrying about the forest to find hollow trees to make their homes in. And *you* will be scurrying about with all the other young creatures who will be hunting for new homes."

"No," Ringtail said, "I'll still live in the old hollow tree by the river! I'll always live there with my father and my mother and my little sister!"

The old Muskrat made no reply to this, and something in his silence made Ringtail a little uneasy.

"I *will* always live in the hollow tree, won't I, Muskrat?" he asked.

"If I were you," the Muskrat said gravely, "I

would not think about that now, for you will understand many things when the winter has passed and the creatures come again. Do not think about it now. It will come in good time."

Ringtail was too troubled to reply. His father had said something like this to him not long ago, he remembered. But he had not thought much about it then.

Could it be that some time he would go away from the hollow tree and hunt a new home? Was this what his father and the old Muskrat had meant to say?

A little breeze stirred the cat-tails and it felt sharp and cold as it riffled through Ringtail's long soft fur. He looked at the old Muskrat lying in the path. There was something else that he wanted to know; something he *had* to know.

"Will I be happy then?" he asked.

"Yes," the Muskrat told him, "you will be happy. You have learned many things since first you came up here to the marsh. You have learned not to be too curious about things you do not understand, and to guard yourself against danger. But these things have not made you unhappy; they have only made you wiser and better able to look after yourself. And that is the way it will be when you waken. You will understand many things, but you will still be happy."

"Thank you for telling me, Muskrat," Ringtail said. "I'll go home now, but I'll come again to the marsh to see you."

"I hope so," the Muskrat answered. "I will watch for you."

For a time after Ringtail had disappeared along the path, the Hermit Muskrat still lay without moving. But at last he got to his feet and limped down to the edge of the bay.

"I must finish mending my roof now," he said, slipping back into the water.

Chapter Thirteen

BEYOND THE WILLOWS

THE winter day dawned gray and cold, and the snow fell steadily, hour after hour, until it covered all the forest.

The pathways were gone, and the brush pile where the little Chipmunks played had disappeared. The great stone near which the old Groundhog used to sit on summer afternoons was now only a round white mound, and even the hard roof of the river was buried under the snow.

The forest itself was silent, and to Ringtail, lying half asleep inside the hollow tree, this silence was more mysterious than the voices that had once come in through the doorway and made him wonder.

What a long time ago that had been. There were no voices now; no voices anywhere.

Opening his eyes, the little Raccoon looked drowsily about the den. "Father," he said in a low voice, "are you asleep?"

"No, Ringtail, I am still awake," the Raccoon father answered.

"Are you frightened?"

"No, I am not frightened."

The Raccoon father's voice was very gentle, and the little Raccoon crept nearer to him.

How calm and fearless his father was. And how strong and big he looked, there in the darkness of the den. A great pride filled Ringtail's heart.

"When I have lived a long time," he whispered, "will I be as brave as you are, Father?"

"You are brave now, Ringtail," his father told him, "and what is better still, you are learning to be wise. You already know many things about the forest and the river."

"And the marsh!" Ringtail added, pleased by his father's praise.

"Yes, and the marsh, too," the old Raccoon said, "and when the long sleep is over, I want you to remember all the things that you have learned."

"About the Dangers, you mean?" Ringtail asked.

"Yes, about the Dangers," his father said.

The little Raccoon lay for a moment looking into the darkness. "I have seen the Mighty One," he said at last, "and the shaggy creature that belongs to him."

The Raccoon father raised his head sharply. "You have seen them?"

"Yes, Father," Ringtail answered. "I saw them come out of the forest, but they did not see me."

"That is well," the old Raccoon said softly. "You must never let them see you, Ringtail."

"Can you tell me how to hide from them, Father?" Ringtail asked anxiously. "Can you tell me what to do?"

The Raccoon father looked at him and noted with pride how strong and sturdy he had grown. "It is hard to know," he said slowly, "but when you hear the voice of the shaggy creature, you must get to the river if you can. The river is your friend and will hide the scent of your footsteps."

"Wouldn't I be safe high in a tree?" Ringtail asked.

"No," his father said, "for the shaggy creature would see you and would stand by the tree and raise his dreadful baying voice until the Mighty One came with his shining stick that kills from a long

way off. No, the forest is not safe. The river is the only place; and though you may have to run a long way, over hills and through gullies, through the tall grass and tangled weeds, *you must reach the river, Ringtail.*"

"I will," Ringtail answered bravely. "I will reach the river."

"I think you will," his father answered, "but when the long sleep is over, remember what I have said. You will need to know these things then, for you will be leaving the hollow tree. You will be going away, and you will be going alone, going to find your own home, just as I found mine."

For a moment Ringtail lay in silence. Now he knew certainly that he would go away and leave the hollow tree! His father had just told him so.

But somehow it did not trouble him as it had when first his father spoke of it to him, or even when the old Muskrat of the marsh had talked to him about it. It only made him wonder.

"Where will I go?" he asked presently.

"I do not know that," the Raccoon father said, "but somewhere in the forest there is a hollow tree— your hollow tree. You will find it, Ringtail."

"Yes," the little Raccoon said drowsily, "I'll find it."

He wished he were not so sleepy now. He would like to go to the doorway of the den and look out once more at the forest. He would like to see again the far-away hills and the clump of willows at the bend of the river. What was beyond the willows? he wondered again, as he had so often wondered before. He had always meant to go there and find out.

Suddenly he raised his head. "Father," he said, "will Little Sister go away too?"

"Yes," his father told him, "she will go. The young always go after the long sleep."

"But won't she be lonely and frightened?"

"No," answered the old Raccoon, "for all through the forest and along the river side there will be other young creatures. Each will find a mate, and together they will make a new home, just as your mother and I made our home in this hollow tree. It will be a glad time for all young creatures everywhere, Ringtail. A glad and happy time."

The old Raccoon did not speak again and after a moment Ringtail stirred uneasily and half rose to his feet. "Father," he said, "won't you tell me more about my hollow tree?"

"Lie down, Ringtail." It was his mother's voice close to his ear. "Father is asleep now and so is Little Sister. The winter is here, and you must sleep too."

Ringtail lay down, but he was not yet quite ready to sleep.

"How will I know when winter is over, Mother?" he asked. "How will I know when it is time to waken?"

"You will hear the voices," she told him. "You have not forgotten the voices, have you, Ringtail? The voices from the Outside World?"

"Oh, no, I remember them," the little Raccoon said, "and I'll be glad to hear them when they come again."

Once more he closed his eyes, but there was still something that he must say.

"Mother, do you know about the wonderful things that I'll do when the voices come again?" he asked.

"Yes, Ringtail."

"I'll go away and find my own hollow tree," he told her. "I already know where it is. No one else knows where it is. Father does not know, and the old Muskrat of the marsh does not know. But I know."

"Yes, Ringtail," his mother said softly. "Hush now, and sleep."

"It is farther than the Groundhog's hollow," the little Raccoon went on, and his voice was now only a tiny whisper. "It is farther than the marsh. I will tell you where it is, Mother. It is beyond the willows! Beyond—the—willows—at—the—bend—of—the—river——"

Softly the Raccoon mother smoothed his furry neck with her tongue.

"Yes, Ringtail," she said again. "Beyond the willows."

And with her nose still resting on little Ringtail's neck, she closed her eyes.

BEYOND THE WILLOWS

The wind blew down from the far-away hills and whistled through the bare branches of the old hollow tree. But the Raccoon family did not mind it.

They did not mind that the little river was cold and still between its banks, or that the snow fell deeper and deeper on forest and meadow.

For safe and warm inside their den, they lay close together in the darkness.

The Coming of the Cold was here. It was time for them to sleep.

THE END.